Green Bean
Green Bean!

By Patricia Thomas
Illustrated by Trina L. Hunner

Dawn Publications

or my bumper crop of new little sprouts: Will, Lily, Brie, Jack, Eli, Anna, Raelyn,
Carma, Maverick, James, Hudson, and Xavier — PT

For Gene and Christine Hunner — TLH

Library of Congress Cataloging-in-Publication Data

Thomas, Patricia, 1934-

Green bean! Green bean! / by Patricia Thomas ; illustrated by Trina L. Hunner. -- First edition.

pages cm

Summary: "A girl plants the seed of a green bean and watches it grow and mature through the seasons, even providing a nook in which to read a book. Includes supplementary information about the life cycle of plants, pertinent vocabulary, and activities"-- Provided by publisher.

ISBN 978-1-58469-543-1 (hardback) -- ISBN 978-1-58469-544-8 (pbk.) [1. Green bean--Fiction. 2. Beans--Fiction. 3. Gardening--Fiction.] I. Hunner, Trina L., illustrator II. Title.

PZ7.T36927Gr 2016

[E]--dc23

2015014688

Book design and computer production by Patty Arnold, *Menagerie Design & Publishing*

Manufactured by Regent Publishing Services, Hong Kong
Printed December, 2015, in ShenZhen, Guangdong, China

10 9 8 7 6 5 4 3 2 1

First Edition

SUNBURST SEEDS

POLE BEANS – Scarlet Runner

Green bean.

Green bean.
And freckles and speckles.

Freckles and speckles.
Soon a root and a shoot.

A root and a shoot.
And a sprout peaking out.

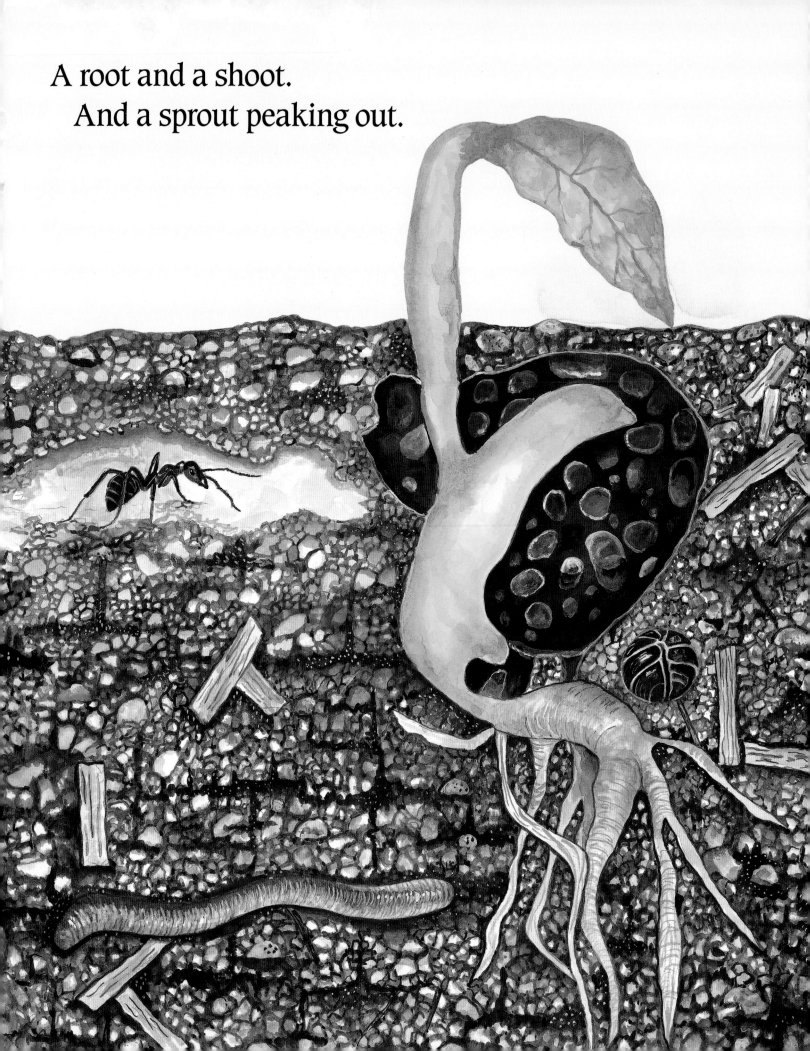

A sprout peeking out.
But a bunch comes for lunch.

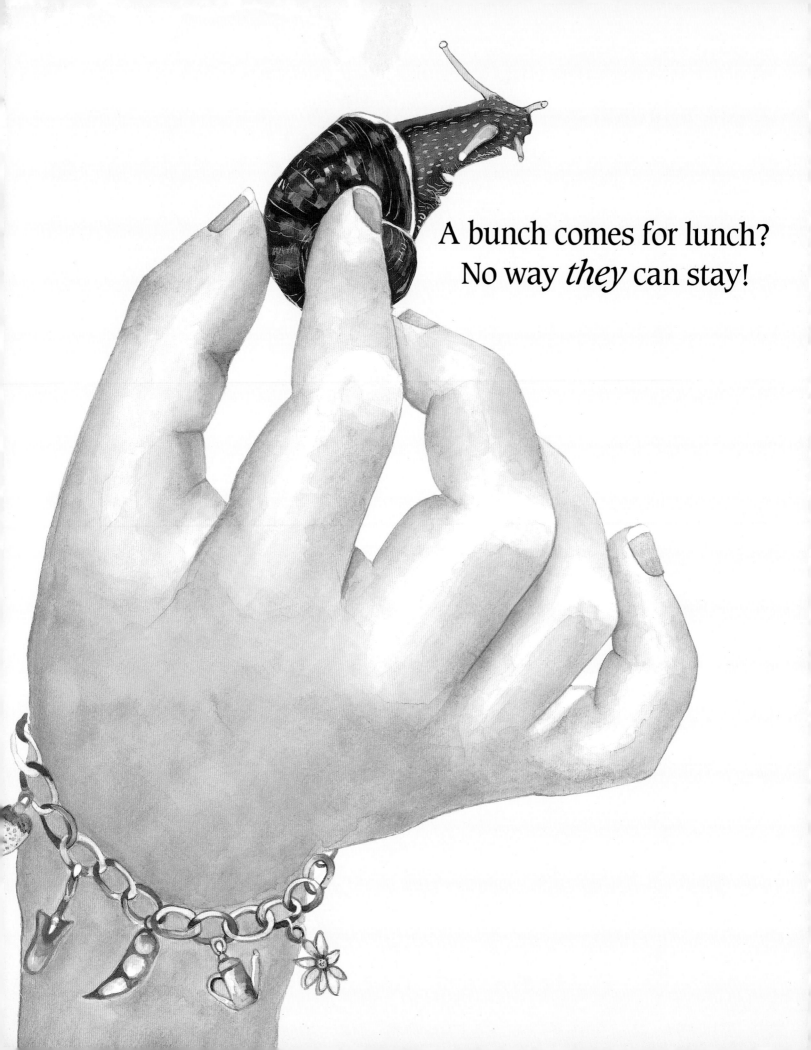

A bunch comes for lunch?
No way *they* can stay!

No way *they* can stay!
Now a hoe to help grow.

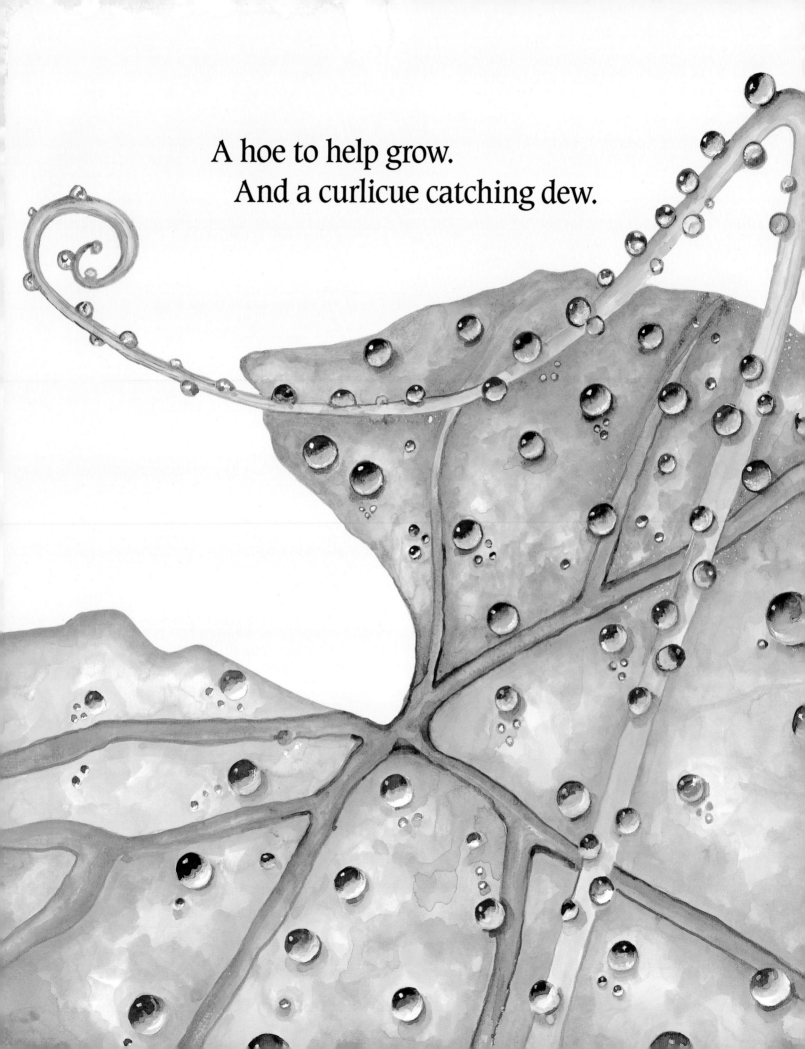

A hoe to help grow.
And a curlicue catching dew.

Curlicue catching dew.
Oh no! Wind roars.
Rain pours.

Wind roars. Rain pours.
But staked tight, stands right.

Staked tight, stands right.
But rabbit could grab it!

Rabbit could grab it.
Stop his threat! Set a net!

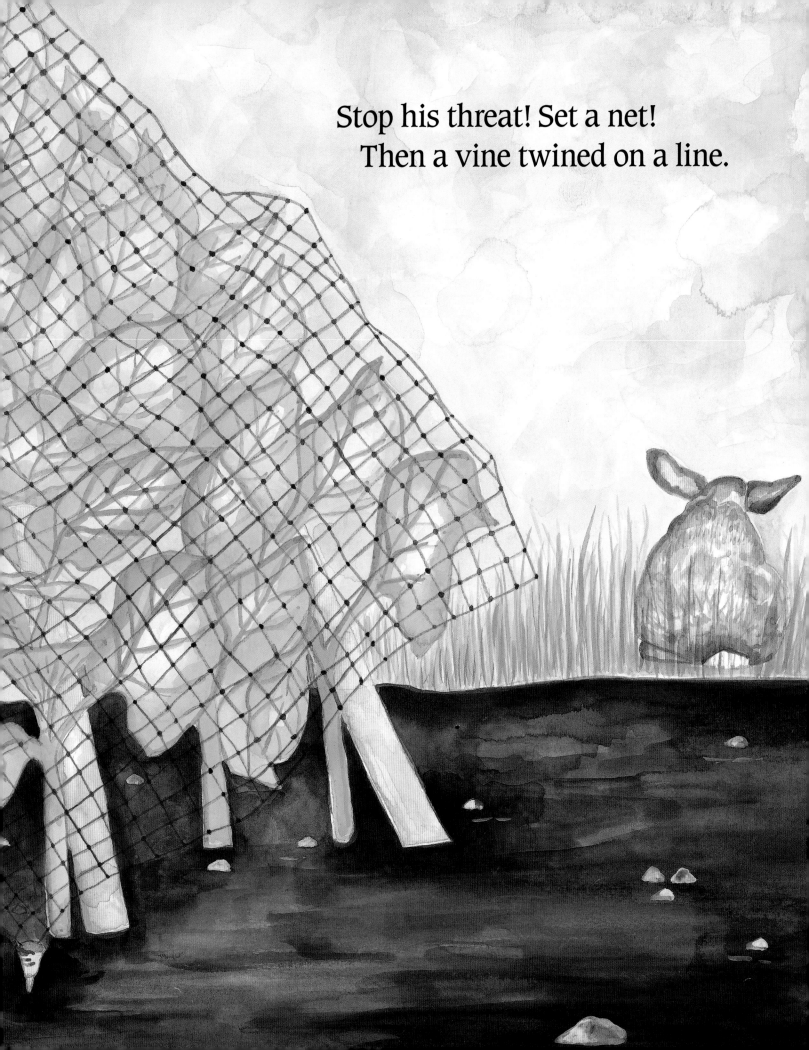

Stop his threat! Set a net!
Then a vine twined on a line.

A vine twined on a line,
And a nook to read a book.

A nook to read a book,
And overhead blossoms red.

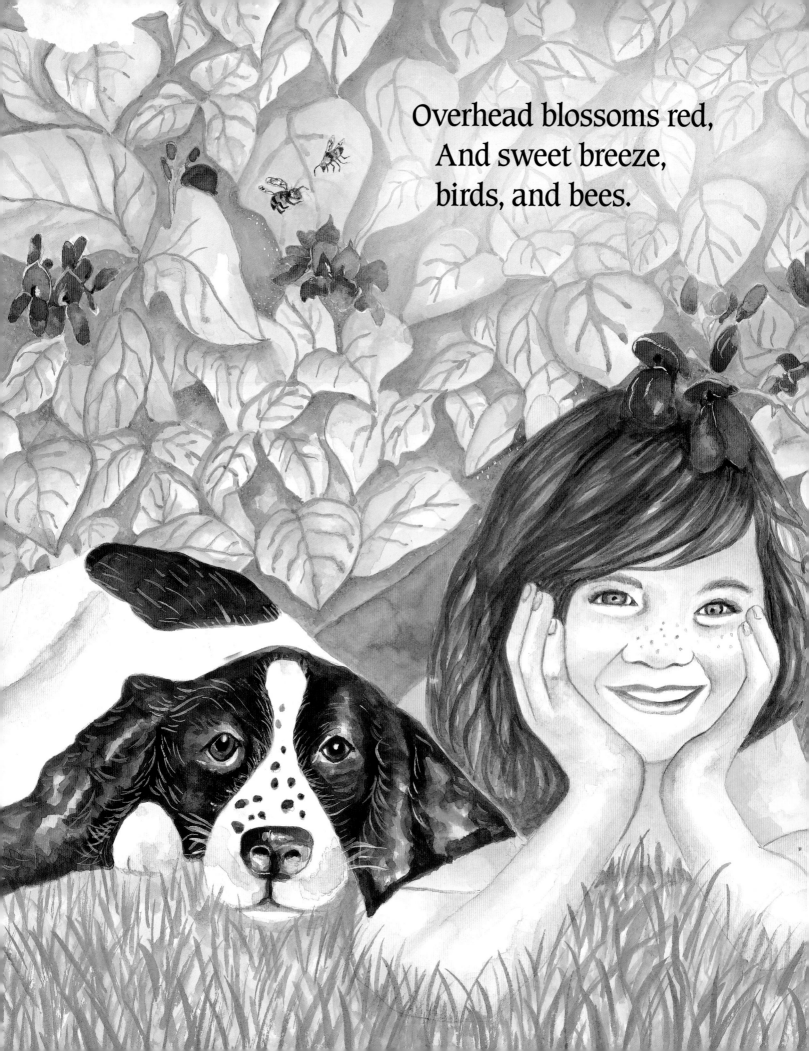

Overhead blossoms red,
And sweet breeze,
birds, and bees.

Sweet breeze, birds, and bees.
And long, lean
bean,
bean,
bean,
bean.

Bean, bean, bean, bean.
Be quick! Lots to pick!

Be quick! Lots to pick!
But one high,
brown and dry.

One high,
brown and dry.
Vine jumbled.
Bean tumbled.

Vine jumbled.
Bean tumbled.
Waits below drifty snow.

Waits below drifty snow
Till warm sun. What fun!

Warm sun. What fun!
And . . .

Green bean!

Green bean!

Green bean!

Green bean!

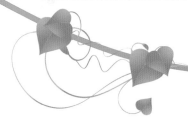

Life Cycle

Green Bean's story starts with a seed. Different seeds grow into different kinds of plants. This story is about a Scarlet Runner Bean. Follow Green Bean's journey through its life cycle.

In warm, moist earth, the seed **germinates** and starts to grow. The seed sends a **root** downward for water and food. It sends a **shoot** upward, looking for sunlight.

A tiny **sprout** peeks above the soil. The **chlorophyll** in its green leaves grabs sunlight.

The sprout grows into a tall plant. The chlorophyll helps the plant change sunlight, water, and air into food through **photosynthesis**.

When the plant blooms, its flowers are filled with **pollen** and sweet-smelling **nectar**. Bees and birds **pollinate** the flowers when they come to drink the nectar. The flowers grow into bean pods filled with beans.

The **beans** inside the ripe pods dry out. Dried beans are the **seeds** that are planted in the spring.

Grow Your Own Green Bean

You can plant your own green bean and watch the amazing cycle yourself.

1. Punch a hole or two in the bottom of a plastic cup and fill it with soil. If you use a clear cup, you can watch the seed as it sprouts and grows.

2. Push a bean down into the soil.

3. Add water just until the soil is damp, and place the cup in a sunny window.

4. Wait and watch what happens. You might want to use a notebook to write down or draw pictures of what you see.

5. When your plant has sprouted and begins to turn into a seedling, plant it outside. First loosen the earth. Then dig a hole and gently slip your plant into it, soil and all. Be careful not to damage the roots. Pack the soil around your plant and water it. Help your plant grow, just like the gardener did in the story.

Words to Know

Germinate *means to grow or develop.* A tiny plant is curled up inside a seed. When this tiny plant cracks though a seed coating and sprouts, it has germinated. Some seeds need to be in the dark to germinate. Some need light. But they all need water and warmth to start to grow.

Chlorophyll *is the substance that makes plants green.* Chlorophyll is more than just a pretty color. It allows plants to collect energy from sunlight to make food.

Photosynthesis *is the way plants make food.* Plants draw water from their roots. They gather carbon dioxide from the air with their leaves. Chlorophyll in the leaves collects energy from sunlight. Plants turn water, carbon dioxide, and sunlight into food through photosynthesis.

Pollen *is a fine powder found inside flowers.* It's found on the tips of slender strands in the center of a flower. Pollen is necessary for a plant to make fruit.

Nectar *is the sweet liquid found inside flowers.* Nectar attracts bees, butterflies and moths, and hummingbirds. Bees use nectar to make honey.

Pollinate *means to spread pollen.* When bees, butterflies and moths, and hummingbirds sip nectar from inside a flower, they pick up powdery pollen on their bodies. They spread the pollen as they fly from flower to flower. If pollen spreads down inside a flower, a "fruit" can start to form. After a bean plant is pollinated, bean pods will start to grow.

Beans and Seasons

Refer to the story and illustrations to find the answers to these questions:

  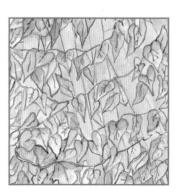 

🌱 What is Green Bean doing in the spring?

🌱 What is Green Bean doing in the summer?

🌱 What is Green Bean doing in the fall?

🌱 What is Green Bean doing in the winter?

🌱 Why does Green Bean change?

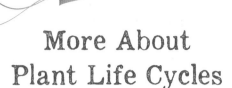

More About Plant Life Cycles

The life story of Green Bean is a marvelous cycle. At first, a plant is just a tiny "dot" lying dormant inside the bean. When it's planted with moisture and the sun's warmth, the plant will **germinate** and start to grow. It sends a **root** downward looking for food and water deep in the soil and anchoring the plant in place. At almost the same time, it sends a tiny **shoot** upward, stretching for the sunlight.

Soon the stem pushes through the soil, and a pale, little **sprout** appears. It may even wear part of the **seed coat** as a cap. At first it seems to have no color at all. But as leaves emerge, **chloroplasts** in their cells produce **chlorophyll**, which gives the plant (now a **seedling**) its green color. The function of chlorophyll is to enable **photosynthesis**—the process by which plants transform energy from the sun, plus water and nutrients (principally carbon dioxide from the air) into sugar. Sugar is stored as food for the plant.

As the seedling gets taller, it grows leaves which help collect more sunlight, and before you know it, that plant is up and growing! Or in this case "off and running," because the Green Bean in the story is a real-life *Scarlet Runner Bean*—a gardener's delight known as an *edible ornamental*. It's a beautiful climbing landscape plant that can cover a wall, shade a patio, or even, as our young gardener discovered, provide a cool little summer hideaway. It also produces a delicious vegetable. The young vine may have to battle insect pests, storms, hungry rabbits, or other critters. Weeds that could choke it need to be hoed or pulled away. But with help from a good gardener, Scarlet Runner Bean will be ready to race up a rope, a pole, a fence, a wall—anything it can grasp with its eager, curling tendrils. It can reach as much as ten feet, bursting out in bright blossoms as it goes!

Hummingbirds, bees, and butterflies, attracted by the sweet nectar of flowers, will come dancing around the blossoms, which are usually red (but are sometimes combinations of white, orange, or pink). While sipping nectar, insects and birds pick up the fine **pollen**, produced by the male part of the flower (**anther**). The anther sits atop slender strands in the flower's center. The pollen is spread to the female part of the flower (**ovary**) deep inside the blossom. Through this process of **pollination** and **fertilization**, flowers turn into long, lovely green beans. When the beans are ripe, they will be ready to eat fresh in summer or to store and enjoy through the winter.

As with any bean, pods may be dried, and the beans inside saved to be planted in the spring to grow a new crop. It's best to dry beans indoors for planting, but sometimes forgotten beans dry out on their own and sink into soft earth, staying dormant until spring rain and sunshine awaken them to begin the cycle all over again.

Anther

Ovary

Fun Things to Do

❀ Spread a variety of seeds on damp paper towels. Slip the paper towels into closed plastic bags or place them in aluminum foil pans covered with plastic wrap to create mini greenhouses. Watch to see how seeds begin to sprout and/or grow roots. Observe how the roots are different in different seeds. Photograph seeds or draw pictures to keep in a notebook.

❀ Create a table centerpiece by assembling a basket or bowl of different fruits and vegetables paired with their seeds. For example, you might use apples/apple seeds, carrots/carrot seeds, beans/bean seeds, or pumpkins/pumpkin seeds.

❀ Serve a snack or lunch with different fruits, vegetables, and edible seeds. You can make a delicious, healthy salad with apples, celery, and sunflower seeds mixed with dressing and put on top of romaine lettuce.

- Take a "seed walk" through the neighborhood. See what kinds of plants you can find and what their seeds look like. How are wild seeds spread and planted? How are they pollinated?

- Create a mosaic by gluing a variety of dry seeds onto a piece of cardboard.

- Plant seeds indoors or outdoors in a garden, flower pot, or raised beds. Experiment by planting the seeds at different depths or at different times and observing when they become seedlings and how the plants grow.

Telling Green Bean's Story

For untold centuries, we have been enjoying, singing, and repeating all sorts of songs, poems, nursery rhymes, fairytales, and folktales that continue to captivate us with their clever cumulative logic—*This is the House that Jack Built, There Was an Old Lady Who Swallowed a Fly, The Gingerbread Man, The Sky is Falling,* and many others. Cumulative tales use repetition and rhythm to create their desired effect. Some rhyme; some do not.

Green Bean, written in a crisp rhyme style, offers a variation of the cumulative form that doesn't actually repeat *all* the elements each time one is added. Because the little bean is ever-changing, the poem follows it through the marvelous, magical stages of its growth, circling all the way back to where the wonderful process begins again—nature's own cumulative, constantly moving cycle.

A Nook to Read a Book and Other Fun

Growing a Book Nook takes planning and patience, but the results are worth the trouble! Carefully choose a spot to grow a hideaway. Decide on the shape for your hideout (a circle works well for creating a teepee) and prepare the soil. Set up a frame of sticks or cords, outlining your shape. For a teepee, sticks should all lean toward the center, like an upside-down ice cream cone. Plant seeds around the base of the frame for plants that vine, such as runner beans and morning glories. Consult your garden store for seeds, care, and planting advice. Tend the plants as they grow, helping their "curlicues" find holds to climb the framework. Tall, non-vining plants, such as sunflowers, can also grow into a cozy, secret book nook. When your "nook" is green and flowering, bring a book into your special summer retreat! No room to grow a book nook? Find ways to create different green hideaways in a backyard, on a rooftop, even in a room with blankets, pillows, and indoor plants.

Once you're in your Book Nook:

- Write a cumulative poem to explain how a different seed or plant grows, such as corn, pea, sunflower, or marigold.

- Make a list of stories with seeds and plants and find books about them to read and share. Some traditional stories are *Jack and the Beanstalk, The Princess and the Pea,* and *The Legend of Johnny Appleseed.*

- Make a circle painting showing each stage of Green Bean's growth.

- With friends, act out Green Bean's story as a Reader's Theater.

Educators: There are many wonderful resources online, including activities and lesson plans. Go to www.dawnpub.com and click on "Activities," or scan this code.

PATRICIA THOMAS grew up on a farm in Pennsylvania where she learned the delight of summers spent barefoot and hands digging in garden dirt. From her teacher parents, she also learned the joy of books, reading, poetry, and rhyme. The gardening part paid off when profits from 4-H tomato projects helped finance tuition at Penn State University. She married her PSU sweetheart, became a copywriter/editor, raised a family, and discovered she was a children's writer. Today, nearly 45 years later, her first book, *Stand Back, Said the Elephant, "I'm Going to Sneeze!"* still sends kids around the world into gales of laughter. Her books, stories, and articles cover wide-ranging poetic and prose styles. She has presented workshops, writing courses, lectures, and teacher-education seminars.

TRINA HUNNER'S favorite way to eat green beans is Szechwan style with lots of ginger, garlic, and chili peppers! Trina began to mark her life around the cycles of the growing season when she and her husband, Nikos, lived next to an organic farm. They now live in the Sierra Nevadas of northern California. Trina's tried growing green beans there, but hasn't had much success—beans just don't grow well under the tall pines that surround their home. Trina has illustrated two other books for Dawn Publications: *Molly's Organic Farm* and *On Kiki's Reef*. When not creating vibrant watercolor paintings, she enjoys biking to the elementary school where she teaches, skiing in the mountains near her home, and playing with her trio of lovable pets.

Also Illustrated by Trina Hunner

Molly's Organic Farm — The true story of a homeless cat that found herself in the wondrous world of an organic farm. Seen through Molly's eyes, the reader discovers the interplay of nature that grows wholesome food.

On Kiki's Reef — A tiny baby sea turtle scrambles across the sandy beach and into the sea. Floating far out in the ocean, Kiki becomes a gentle giant and ends up with a fascinating community of creatures on a coral reef.

A Few Other Nature Awareness Books from Dawn

Jo MacDonald Had a Garden. E-I-E-I-O! Young Jo, granddaughter of Old MacDonald, discovers the delights of a garden—and also the pond and woods on the farm, in *Jo MacDonald Saw a Pond* and *Jo MacDonald Hiked in the Woods.*

What's in the Garden? — Good food doesn't come from a store shelf. It begins with a garden bursting with life! Discover the variety of fruits and veggies waiting for you in the garden, and get kid-friendly recipes to start a lifetime of good eating.

If You Love Honey — It takes ALL of nature to make the sweetest of treats—delicious golden honey. From honey bees in the field to earthworms underground and everything in-between, explore the intertwining food web of plants and animals.

Pitter and Patter — Follow two raindrops, Pitter and Patter, as they take different paths through the watershed. A water drop is a wonderfully adventurous thing to be!

Dawn Publications is dedicated to inspiring in children a deeper understanding and appreciation for all life on Earth. You can browse through our titles, download resources for teachers, and order at www.dawnpub.com or call 800-545-7475.